Desert Rose

PRAISE FOR *STORYSHARES*

"One of the brightest innovators and game-changers in the education industry."
– Forbes

"Your success in applying research-validated practices to promote literacy serves as a valuable model for other organizations seeking to create evidence-based literacy programs."

- Library of Congress

"We need powerful social and educational innovation, and Storyshares is breaking new ground. The organization addresses critical problems facing our students and teachers. I am excited about the strategies it brings to the collective work of making sure every student has an equal chance in life."
– Teach For America

"Around the world, this is one of the up-and-coming trailblazers changing the landscape of literacy and education."
- International Literacy Association

"It's the perfect idea. There's really nothing like this. I mean wow, this will be a wonderful experience for young people."   - Andrea Davis Pinkney, Executive Director, Scholastic

"Reading for meaning opens opportunities for a lifetime of learning. Providing emerging readers with engaging texts that are designed to offer both challenges and support for each individual will improve their lives for years to come. Storyshares is a wonderful start."
- David Rose, Co-founder of CAST & UDL

Desert Rose

Tamuna Tsertsvadze

STORYSHARES

Story Share, Inc.
New York. Boston. Philadelphia.

Storyshares
Story Share, Inc.
24 N. Bryn Mawr Avenue #340
Bryn Mawr, PA 19010-3304
www.storyshares.org

Inspiring reading with a new kind of book.

Interest Level: High School
Grade Level Equivalent: 4

9781642615258

Book design by Storyshares

Printed in the United States of America

Storyshares Presents

1

They used to play together. They were best friends. It didn't matter that they belonged to different tribes from different countries.

She was born in Endon. Endon was a country of waving grass, evergreen trees, flowering fields, clear waters, and chirping birds. The sky was blue and the sun always shone. She lived in a hut near the great Assouh River. She had everything her heart could desire: a loving family, peace, and happiness. Her name was Orchidea.

He was from Alib, the vast, golden desert. Alib had many wild camels, cactuses, and poisonous insects. This desert had nothing in material wealth, but it was home to many tribes.

He belonged to one of these tribes—the strongest one, called Ahaud. The Ahaud tribe had mighty tribesmen, strong weaponry, many camels and tents, and a little white city near a tiny oasis. The Ahaud boy was called Roziel.

The Endonians worshipped seven gods. The mightiest and highest god was called Endon. He was the great peacekeeper. The Endonians didn't pray to Endon and the six other gods all day and night. Instead, the gods were thought of as illusionary beings who lived high up in the sky.

The Alibians, including members of the Ahaud tribe, believed in only one god: mighty Sahad, the father of all. The vast desert had little to offer. While travelling through the never-ending sand, the Alibians prayed to the great Sahad. The Ahauds, and all the Alibians, loved their god.

These two children, though completely different, still found common interests. They were both children, they were both human, and they both loved to play. So when the boy's tribesmen travelled through the desert and arrived at the Assouh River, the boy would often meet the girl there. He would cross the river to hold her hand. Although it was forbidden, they would play together.

It did not matter to the children that their friendship was forbidden. Endonians and Alibians hated each other. They were often at war. Alibians attacked Endonian shores, killing the people and taking their goods. Endonians would hang Alibians in public as revenge.

This war lasted for centuries. It all began because of their religious differences. The Alibians thought the Endonians had little faith. The Endonians thought that the Alibians had only faith and nothing more. So they never accepted each other.

But Orchidea and Roziel were just children. They knew little about these religious differences—or any differences. They saw each other as normal humans. In fact, they thought they were quite similar. Both of them had two eyes, two hands, two feet, and the will to play.

So what if they spoke different languages? Their games didn't need any language. So what if they were different genders? Their games could be played by anyone. So what if they were of different nationalities? Their games didn't concern national affairs. To play their games, they just needed one thing: each other.

And they had each other once a week, when the Ahaudian tribe arrived at the Assouh River for water. After a day, the tribe would continue on its way.

So every week they played, smiling, giggling, and having fun. That was all they needed.

2

"Roziel, wait! You're too fast!"

Eight-year-old Orchidea chased after Roziel. Older by four years, he was much faster.

"Haha, try and catch me, Orchid!" The red-haired boy giggled and rushed onward.

The children played on the shores of the large, clean river. They raced through the tall, green grass spotted with flowers. Beyond the grasses sat little wooden huts. The other side of the river was covered with golden sand. It was barren except for the white tents of the desert nomads.

Orchidea caught up with Roziel, who intentionally slowed his pace. She ran at him, making him fall into the grass. They both laughed. Orchidea giggled and put a flower crown on the boy's head. Roziel chuckled.

"What's this? A rose crown?" he asked.

"Yes! It makes your red hair even more beautiful!" Orchidea giggled and reached out to touch the hair she loved so much.

"Thank you!" Roziel beamed and softly fingered the rose petals.

Suddenly they heard a voice from the other side of the river. "Roziel, get over here! We're leaving!"

Hearing this, both children sighed.

"Well, here you are again, leaving . . ." Orchidea looked down sadly.

"Hey! But I'll be back, won't I?" Roziel kneeled beside her, hugging her tightly. "And when I'm back we can play hide-and-seek in that evergreen forest. The one with the flowers we love so much. Right?" She giggled, and he smiled. "See you later, tiny!"

Orchidea watched her friend cross the bridge of the Assouh River and run up to his family. They were clothed in white from head to toe, even their faces were covered. Only the guns they bore weren't white.

Orchidea watched as Roziel jumped onto his camel and followed his family into the vast desert. She didn't move until Roziel's white cloak disappeared behind the golden horizon.

3

Sunday came. Orchidea knew very well what this meant.

"It is Sahad Day! Roziel will come!" she cried and leaped up from her bed. She dressed quickly and rushed out to the river shore. She looked out at the vast desert on the other side of the river. She waited for him, just like she always did.

Her eyes widened with joy as he appeared. He came with his camel and his nomadic family, as he usually did. But there was something different about him.

Roziel, who always wore his hair bushy and long, now had it tied in a low ponytail. He looked more grown up, and he wore different clothes. His expression was sad instead of cheerful.

Orchidea became worried. What did this mean? Did something happen? Was something wrong?

Roziel slowly crossed the wooden bridge on his camel and approached Orchidea.

"Roziel!" Orchidea jumped happily.

"Hello, Orchid," he said somberly.

"Wh . . . What's wrong, Roziel? Did anything happen?"

"Actually . . . yes." Roziel sighed. "The thing is . . . this must be our last meeting, tiny."

"What? Why?!" Orchidea asked. Tears came to her eyes.

"They . . . they said I must become a prophet. I don't really understand why, but I must move far away from here. I can never even see my own tribe. They will take me to a building in the center of our desert, in the Cloister of Sahad. I must study there."

"So you're going to school? That's awful!" Orchidea exclaimed.

"It is not a school, exactly. It is a monastery, but both men and women live there. They pray to the Great Sahad, our god, every day and every night. There the prophet of Sahad must sit. There is a prophet in every generation. The prophet is chosen by a special sign: red hair.

"In the Alibian tribes, no person has red hair. It is extremely rare and occurs only once every generation. The one with red hair has the skills of a prophet. That is what the elders told me. And that means . . ." he sighed. "That means I'm going far away. I'm really sad, Orchid. I will miss you."

He stepped down from his camel to hug her.

"But . . . but . . . we didn't even get to play hide-and-seek!" Orchid said through her tears. "You . . . you promised, Roziel!" She was sobbing. "I will miss you so much! You're my only friend! Please don't go!"

Roziel sighed again. "I'm sorry. I'm so sorry, Orchid."

They held each other, squeezing each other as if wanting to exchange all the love they had in their hearts. And then, Roziel felt the soft touch of a petal on his palm. He looked down and saw that the little girl had handed him a deep red rose.

"What's this?" Roziel asked.

"A rose," Orchidea said. "I want to gift it to you as a goodbye. I want you to remember that I will always keep our memories and our friendship in my heart. Please don't forget me, Roziel." Tears ran down her cheeks. "I know that roses do not grow in the desert. But I believe this one will never fade. It is entwined with my feelings. You will always be my best friend, Roziel. Always."

Roziel smiled. He wiped away the girl's tears with his fingers and hugged her again, taking the rose.

"Thank you, Orchid," he said quietly. Then he stepped back and mounted his camel.

Orchidea watched him cross the bridge and gallop away. Soon only his cloudy white cloak could be seen on the horizon. Then it too disappeared.

4

Years passed. Orchidea grew. From a loving and playful child, she turned into a beautiful and charming young woman. She had everything she needed: a loving family, close friends, and the flowering fields and evergreen forests she loved so much. Somewhere deep in her heart was the memory of a young desert nomad. Though the memory of what he looked like faded, she didn't forget his friendship. She knew that somewhere deep in the desert, he still lived.

But she dived into her own affairs and had little time to dream of Roziel. She was learning that life wasn't all fun and games.

The war between Endonians and Alibians worsened. From minor attacks, it turned into a true conflict. The Endonians were going to send troops to the desert to exterminate the whole Alibian nation.

Instead of waiting for an attack, the Alibians closed in on the Assouh River. Armed guards shot anyone who stepped onto their golden sand.

Eventually, the Endonians lost the war. They had to pay five hundred thousand gold pieces to the Alibians, which they could not afford. So they came to an agreement with Alibian authorities. Instead, they would pay one hundred thousand gold pieces, plus one thousand young women who would become slaves. This horrible outcome enraged the Endonian population, but they could do nothing.

So the price was paid. One thousand poor souls were sent across the river to the heartless terrorists. And these girls were not from big Endonian cities, but from rural areas—the tiny huts of the countryside. Thus, one of these young women happened to be Orchidea.

She cried and yelled but was still taken off her home. She was not even being able to bid her family a proper goodbye. She was heartlessly taken across the river, rejected by her own nation, separated from her mother, father, and brother. She was filled with dread. She cried for days and nights over the loss of her beloved life.

She prayed to Endon now, to let her get home. As she fell into despair, Endon was her only hope.

Desert Rose

5

"Hey, maiden, get me a glass of wine!"

Many filthy men gathered in the pub on the oasis. It was one of the most popular places in the desert. The men were drunk, singing and yelling. There was turmoil in the pub. The waitresses had whip marks and scars all over their bodies.

One of the waitresses, a fair, dark-haired maid, brought a glass of wine to the drunken man who had asked for it. She wore red, nomadic clothes and her belly was uncovered. It was Orchidea.

After setting down the drink, she turned to leave. But the drunk grabbed her arm and grinned, showing his yellow teeth.

"Amuse me, lass," he demanded. He reached for her lips, but she shrieked and slapped him.

"Ah!" the man cried and rubbed his cheek. "How dare you!" He grabbed his whip. The girl moved to escape, but two other men caught her and made her kneel.

Tears welled in the maiden's eyes. She prepared for the pain. The man lifted his whip and hit her. A shriek was heard. And another. And ten more.

"That will teach you a lesson," the man grunted. Then he cried, "Be punished by the name of Sahad, as he forbids women to disobey men!"

"Then curse your Sahad!!" Orchidea exclaimed, tears pouring down her cheeks.

Hearing this, everyone in the bar gasped.

"How dare you insult our god!" said the owner of the pub, who was standing at the counter nearby. He rushed up to the girl and took out his gun. "You don't deserve to live!" he shouted. He was about to pull the trigger when a tall man, covered head to toe in white, approached.

"Do not shoot her," said the nomad. "The ones who insult mighty Sahad should be punished accordingly. Shooting her to death would be too easy. She must be tormented for what she has done. I say we torture her to death!"

"Yeah!" the crowd whooped and yelled.

Orchidea's eyes widened in fear. She couldn't endure such pain. She had already endured too much! She fought free of the men and ran from the pub.

"Hey! Quickly, after her!" the nomads yelled. They rushed out of the pub and mounted their camels.

The exhausted woman couldn't outrun the camels. Soon the nomads caught up with her and captured her again.

"She insults us shamelessly again and again! I won't bear this!" one of the men yelled as he prepared his weapon.

"We could take her to Sahadkhar and give her to the priests for judgment?" one of the nomads suggested.

Hearing this, all the other men laughed.

"Off we go!" they declared happily.

They attached Orchidea's tied hands to one of the camels and went towards the capital oasis of their vast desert—Sahadkhar.

Orchidea had lived as a slave in the desert for a long time. She knew what going to Sahadkhar meant for slaves. They would be judged by Sahad's priests. Those priests were the most evil-hearted men in all the world. They often sentenced people they found guilty to be tortured to death. And their torture methods were unparalleled.

She realized that she was doomed. Tears poured from her eyes, and she shivered.

6

Orchidea was led through the white city on a donkey. Her hands were tied. The citizens called her ugly names. They threw dirt and stones at her as she passed. They demanded that she be tortured and killed.

Armed men on camels accompanied her, their guns at the ready if she dared to escape. She uttered no words. She knew it would be in vain. Tears streamed down her cheeks, dropping onto the sand.

The procession arrived at a tall white building. It had a golden roof and a sun statue on top of it. It was the Cloister of Sahad—the biggest cloister in the Alib desert.

The nomads got off their camels and exchanged some words with the guards. Then they took the girl off the donkey and dragged her inside.

Orchidea was brought in front of a throne. In it sat a man in black robes. His beard was also black. She knew he must be the High Priest. Men in gray robes, the monks, sat on pillows on the floor.

"What has brought you here?" the High Priest asked the nomads.

"Sire, this disgraceful maid dared to insult our god, the Great Sahad. We came here to hear your judgment upon her," one of the nomads answered. He and the other nomads bowed, and they made the girl kneel too. Orchidea looked down at the floor, her lips trembling.

"Hmm . . . Let me see her face," the High Priest ordered.

The nomads stood. One of them, the one with the gun, grabbed the girl by the hair and lifted her head. The girl moaned and looked up at the priest.

He was ugly, but she was in worse shape. There were scars and wounds all over her face. One of her eyes was black and blue. The priest grinned wickedly, seeing how the girl had already been punished.

"What exactly did she say about our god?" he asked.

"She cursed him, sire," the nomads said.

"Did she now?" The priest rose from his throne. "Cut her to pieces with the hot iron! I will not tolerate such disgrace against the Great Sahad!"

"No! Let me go!" Orchidea cried. She tried to struggle free but could not. The men holding her were too strong. When she saw the executioner approach with the hot iron, she froze.

"No!" she cried. "No, I beg you!"

"It is too late now. You should have thought before you loosened your tongue," one of the nomads said.

"No! Get off me!" Orchidea shrieked as the executioner approached.

The iron touched her right arm. She screamed in pain. The nomads were grinning.

As the executioner moved to put the iron on her left arm too, a gray-clothed monk ran into the room.

"His holiness has awoken!" cried the monk. He looked worried. "Who's shrieking so loudly? His holiness is angry. He wants the peace-breaker brought to his room immediately!"

"It was this filthy rat!" said the High Priest, pointing to the girl. "She insulted our god, so we wanted to punish her!"

"Well then, it makes her a double sinner," the gray-robed priest said. "Bring her to his holiness!"

Instantly, the nomads grabbed Orchidea and dragged her to the upper floors. She didn't object anymore. She had no strength left.

She was brought to a splendid white door. The door opened, and they threw the girl inside. She fell to her knees as the door closed. Only the monk entered with her. The room was dim. She could see nothing beyond the dark curtains in front of her.

The monk bowed slightly and spoke to someone behind the curtains. "Your holiness, I brought your disturber. She was being punished for cursing the Great Sahad."

"Leave us alone," came a voice.

The monk bowed and walked out, closing the door.

A man in white robes approached her. His fingers were adorned with golden rings inlaid with big red gems. He had long red hair and expressive green eyes. His eyes were painted and shaded with kohl.

"H . . . have mercy . . ." she whispered, sobbing. "I . . . I beg you . . ."

She covered her face with her beaten hands and started crying bitterly. She was sure she would die. This man wouldn't spare her.

But suddenly, she felt a soft touch on her cheek. Startled, she looked up. The man knelt before her. She saw kindness in his eyes.

"Poor soul. What they have done to you?" he whispered. "Do not fear. I won't harm you."

He smiled and handed her something soft. She looked down at it and gasped. It was a beautiful red rose, blooming like the ones back in her homeland.

Tears came to her eyes when she recalled her home. Then she froze, remembering . . .

She looked at the man again and gasped. No . . . Could it be?

"Is that you?" she murmured through her beaten lips. "Is that really you?"

"Calm down, tiny. Everything's okay now."

Roziel embraced her, and she fell against his chest, hot tears wetting his robes.

7

When she woke, she found that she was lying in a soft golden bed. The blankets were puffy and white. She felt calm. Outside the window, she could see the breeze playing with the sand in the vast desert.

She sighed. Desert again. She had so many horrible memories of the cruel desert. And yet here, in the middle of it, was her savior. Roziel.

As if the thought had called him, he entered, beaming. He examined her wounds and bandaged them with his soft hands.

"Thank you," she said. This sort of kindness was foreign to her after so many years of slavery.

"Don't mention it, tiny." He sat on the edge of the bed and stroked her hair.

Orchidea gulped. She wanted to ask something but was hesitant. In the past, questions brought only beatings. But her growling stomach won her over. She slowly touched the boy's open palm.

"Y . . . your holiness . . ."

"Please, Orchidea, call me Roziel. I still value our old friendship more than anything."

"Roziel," she said hesitantly. "I feel hungry. Please . . ." She looked at him for a reaction. She'd had years of bad experiences with Alibians. Though she knew Roziel as a boy, she didn't know how he might have changed.

Seeing the fear on her face, the boy's heart grew heavy. He sighed. "Please, Orchid, do not fear me. I shall do everything I can to help you."

He smiled and rang a bell. A nun came in. He ordered her to bring some tea and date fruit cookies for the girl. The nun bowed and walked out.

"Thank you, Roziel," she whispered. Her heart filled with gratitude.

The young man beamed and kissed her softly on the forehead. "You're welcome," he said.

Soon the nun returned with breakfast. Orchidea ate greedily. She couldn't believe how good the cookies tasted, and the tea calmed her. Once finished, she sighed in relief, full and almost happy.

Roziel sat with her. He looked at her as he did when they were children, the girl he loved so much. He had kept her in his heart all this time.

They had finally been reunited. This time, nothing could force them to part.

Desert Rose

Tamuna Tsertsvadze

8

Soon, under Roziel's care, Orchidea managed to overcome her anxieties. She turned once more into the calm, collected girl she once was.

Although the wounds healed, the scars remained. She stayed close to Roziel and relied on him for protection. Around other monks in the cloister or people in the city, she nervously hid behind him.

Orchidea noticed that Roziel had grown into a fine man—he was kind-hearted, mild, and friendly. When it came to justice, however, he could be strict and fierce. He was feared by everyone around him.

One day, when Orchidea was in her room—the room where Roziel often meditated—she noticed a black-covered book on the floor. It was resting on a cloth in front of the pillow where Roziel often sat to meditate.

She curiously looked at the book's title. It said *Sahadia*. *Sahadia* was the sacred book of the Alibians. It contained the story of Sahad, the mighty god. Interested, she began reading.

After reading for two hours, she gasped in shock—she had come upon a great Alibian secret.

She quickly closed the book and stood up. She didn't want anyone to know she'd been reading the book. Non-believers were forbidden from reading it. Leaving the room, she ran right into Roziel.

"Roziel, I—"

"You were reading *Sahadia*?" the boy asked calmly.

"I'm sorry . . ."

"And what did you find out?" Roziel asked.

"I . . . nothing."

Roziel smiled. "No, you did read something, didn't you? I can see it on your face. You're astounded."

The girl sighed, seeing that she couldn't hide anything from the boy. She looked down.

"So that is what Sahad's first prophet was hiding . . ." she murmured. "That your god is identical to Saod—the second name of Endon. The highest of the seven gods. That is how he was . . ." She hesitated, then said, "That is how Sahad was created."

Roziel beamed. "Yes."

"So you don't believe in him?" Orchidea was astonished.

"I do," Roziel answered, "but I also believe in the fact that different names do not matter. The individual is one—the god is one. We have the same god, though we name it differently."

"Yes . . . That is true . . . So the whole war is senseless!" she exclaimed. "But . . . but why don't all the Alibians know this?"

"Because they can't read that book. That version of *Sahadia* is forbidden. Only prophets can read it, but the prophets wanted to manipulate people's minds. So they used their knowledge for personal gain. It gave them power. I, on the other hand, want to prove to everyone how wrong they are." He frowned. "I want to reveal this secret."

"But . . . but what if they don't understand you? What if they turn against you?" she asked, worried.

Roziel smiled. "They will understand . . . We will make them understand." He touched her cheek.

Orchidea smiled too. "I will help you any way that I can," she whispered.

So the friends decided to take measures into their own hands.

9

The Endonian government was greatly concerned.

"The Alibian desert is becoming a dangerous place," one of the newly assigned ministers, Mr. Endopauer, noted. "Alibians have turned against each other. Two opposing groups have formed in Alib. One is led by the tribe of Ahaud, the strongest tribe in Alib. The second is led by Hashad, the biggest tribe in Alib.

"Their war seems to be religiously based. Ahaudians claim that the god Sahad is connected with one of our gods, Endon. They say that Sahad bears Endon's second name, Saod, which is altered by Alibian letters. The Hashadians disagree with this idea. They claim that Sahad is an independent god and has nothing to do with Endon.

"I think this war of theirs is a great opportunity for us to retrieve the poor maidens we sent there years ago. Endonian children belong here, in Endon, not there in the empty desert with those heartless people."

"Mr. Endopauer, we know you are greatly concerned because your daughter was sent to Alib. However, I think we should stick to our own issues now," the Prime Minister, Mr. Riben, said.

"I disagree," said the third minister, Mrs. Elisse. "The fate of those poor maidens concerns us all. They are Endonians, and they are suffering. I say we offer to help the Ahaudians with their war in exchange for our maidens."

"And why should we help the Ahaudians, Mrs. Elisse?" The fourth minister, Mr. Ross, raised an eyebrow.

"Because Ahaudians claim that their god is connected with ours. If we let that opinion prevail, we might be able to build positive diplomatic relationships," Mrs. Elisse explained.

"And keep in mind the fact that the chief of Ahaudians, Sheh Roziel Shehhez, is the current prophet of Sahad," Mr. Endopauer added.

Mr. Riben and Mr. Ross thought for a moment. Then they nodded, accepting the proposal. Mrs. Elisse and Mr. Endopauer smiled.

I'll get you out, Orchidea, Mr. Endopauer thought.

10

"Assemble!"

In the dunes, two armies of nomads gathered.

On one side stood the Ahaudian tribe with its allies, holding guns and pistols.

On the other side stood the Hashadian tribe with its allies, also holding guns.

The thunderous voice that cried through the golden desert belonged to the Ahaudian chief, Sheh Ismael Shehhez. He was a black-haired, brown-eyed man. He was well armed.

On the enemy side was the Hashadian leader—a middle-aged, bald, black-bearded man—Sheh Hussein Omash. He, too, was well armed.

Sheh Ismael cried furiously, "Brothers and sisters, attack!"

The Ahaud allies yelled and knelt as well. They fired their weapons, aiming at the enemy's front lines.

"Attack!" Sheh Hussein likewise cried. The Hashad army and allies began shooting as well.

A terrible slaughter ensued. The soldiers tried to hide behind the dunes, but the bullets still reached them. Each side suffered heavy damage but continued fighting. It seemed as though this terrible fight had no end.

11

"But you can't go there! They will kill you!" Orchidea cried. "A war has started! They won't listen to you!"

"If they don't, then so be it. I will die trying," Roziel said firmly.

"Roziel, I cannot live without you!" Orchidea sobbed. She hugged him desperately, wetting his chest with tears. "Don't leave me again. I lost you for so many years. Now that I've found you, I couldn't bear to lose you again."

Roziel looked down at her and sighed. He took her chin in his hand, tilted her head up, and touched her lips with his.

Orchidea embraced him, but all too soon, Roziel stepped back. "I'm sorry, but I must go. This is for my people. I'm a prophet. It is my duty to serve my people and the truth of my god."

And so he left her in the tower, heading to the battlefields.

Orchidea waited. Every day, she gazed out the tower window, hoping to see Roziel return. After many months, she saw the distant shape of people on the horizon.

She ran outside to meet them as they approached. All of their faces were somber. They were in mourning. To Orchidea's dismay, she noticed that they carried Roziel on a stretcher. He was dead.

Roziel bravely, perhaps foolishly, had tried to intervene amidst the warfare. He tried to explain that the war would not solve any problems. After all, he was the prophet of both tribes. But the Hashadian chief shot Roziel where he stood.

The Ahaudians killed the chief in turn, and then the war was over. But their prophet was dead.

Orchidea, realizing she had lost her best friend, protector, and lover, fell to her knees. She wept all day and all night.

Roziel was placed on his bed in his chamber of his tower. All the Alibians mourned for days.

But the worst was yet to come, and it happened in the months after Roziel's death. No new prophet appeared. No child was born with red hair.

Alibians became concerned. They called a summit to discuss what would happen next.

"It is obvious. My brother was the prophet of Sahad," Sheh Ismael declared. He was Roziel's younger brother. "He died by Hashadian hands—Alibian hands. That means we refused Sahad's protection and denied his truth. Sahad is telling us we should reconsider our attitude towards Endonians. He wants us to know that he is indeed Endon."

"Then why was that book hidden from us for such a long time?" an Ahaudian elder asked doubtfully.

"Isn't it obvious, Sheh Batur?" Ismael inquired. "The priests controlled us by their own intentions. Roziel wanted to free us from that burden, but we didn't let him. If we had listened to Roziel instead of allowing him to be killed, I'm sure a new prophet would have appeared—after Roziel died a peaceful death far in the future. The absence of a new prophet is a sign. Sahad is angry with us for what we did."

The chiefs and elders discussed the matter for a long time. In the end, Ismael's opinion won the debate. They concluded that they had wronged their own god.

So the Alibians set up diplomatic talks with the Endonians. They even agreed to return the one thousand slave maidens they had taken years ago. The women returned to their families and rejoiced.

But Orchidea did not return to Endon with the other women. She remained in Roziel's chamber, weeping for her lost love.

Mr. Endopauer asked the Alibians of his daughter's affairs. At his request, the Alibians removed Orchidea from Roziel's bed against her will. They returned her to Endon, where her saddened family met her with open arms.

Orchidea loved her family, but she remained sad. She could never forget Roziel, her desert rose.

12

Minister Endopauer's house was full of different noblemen, all dressed in formal clothes. It was the day that his daughter, Orchidea Endopauer, would choose her future husband.

The hall was full of people. They drank, talked, and celebrated. Mr. Endopauer talked joyously with his guests, but Orchidea remained in her room. She was not in a celebratory mood. She didn't want to marry. She wanted to go to a convent and spend the rest of her life praying to Endon. She knew she could not find love again. And yet she felt that it was her duty to her parents to go through with this marriage.

A servant entered Orchidea's room. "Everyone's waiting for you, miss."

Orchidea sighed and went out to the hall, glancing at the young men. Her heart sank. She walked up to her parents and looked at her father.

"Are you ready, dear?" Mr. Endopauer asked with a smile.

"Yes, father," she replied as calmly as she could.

"Thank you all for coming!" the minister said to the large crowd. "Now my daughter is going to choose her groom!"

Everyone looked at Orchidea. She stood there motionless, holding back tears. No face stood out to her. Then she recalled that her father wanted to establish a relationship with the Prime Minister, Mr. Riben. So she decided that she would choose Mr. Riben's son.

As she prepared to announce this, guards swiftly entered the room. One of them approached Mr. Endopauer.

"Sir," said the guard. "Alibian ambassadors have come to visit. The United Alibian Empire's new emperor and the highest monk wish to see you."

Hearing this unusual declaration, all of the people began to whisper. They thought that Mr. Endopauer must be very highly regarded among the Alibians if their emperor was attending this celebration. Mr. Endopauer was surprised, but he tried not to show it. He hadn't been expecting this visit at all.

After the establishment of peace on Alibian lands, Alibian tribes allied with each other and formed a huge and powerful country, the United Alibian Empire. The new ruler was named an emperor.

"Um, let them in, please," Mr. Endopauer ordered. He knew that turning away the Alibians after finally establishing peace would be foolish.

Soon the Alibian delegation entered. Five white-clothed men brought in a young man. He was also clothed in white, but he wore a blue scarf over his head—the sign of an emperor.

The Alibians and the Endonians bowed to each other in greeting.

"I'm so glad to welcome you into my house, your majesty!" Mr. Endopauer exclaimed.

"Thank you for the warm welcome," the emperor answered. "I heard that you called all the young Endonian men for a chance at your daughter's hand in marriage. I wanted to try my luck since we're at peace now. I hope you don't mind," he humbly declared.

Hearing this, all of the people began whispering again. The emperor wished to marry Orchidea?

Mr. Endopauer was shocked as well. His whole family, along with himself, were pleased. If Orchidea chose this man, she could become the queen of the Alibian Empire!

Mr. Endopauer spoke quietly to his daughter. "Now Orchid, please choose wisely. You have such a huge opportunity before you!"

He turned back to the emperor. "I'm greatly honored, your majesty. Of course you may participate."

Orchidea became angry. How dare they talk about her like that, as if she was just a prize to be won!

She raised her voice. "I don't wish to marry anyone! Thank you and goodbye!" She stormed out of the hall.

Mr. Endopauer was perplexed. He reddened with shame and embarrassment. What would this whole crowd think of her behavior?

"Oh, I'm so sorry," he said to the guests. "I . . . I'm sure she didn't mean it that way. She's very distraught. I'll talk to her right away." As he was about to follow Orchidea, the Alibian emperor stopped him.

"Please, let me speak with her. Before I was emperor, when Orchidea resided in Alib, we knew each other. Perhaps I can make her reconsider," he said.

Mr. Endopauer looked back at the mysterious man. "Oh, of course, your majesty. As you wish."

"Thank you."

The emperor made his way to Orchidea's room and knocked on her door. The servant immediately reported the visitor to Orchidea. She consented to let the emperor in, for she knew that if she refused, it would only enrage her father.

"Greetings, Miss Endopauer . . ." the emperor said as he entered.

"What do you want from me?" the girl sobbed. "I don't want to get married."

"Well, I just wanted to return a gift. I think you need it more than I do," he said softly. He reached out to place something in her hand.

She looked down and saw a golden ring with a red gem shining on the boy's finger. In his palm was a bright red rose.

Her widened eyes in shock. This rose . . . This hand . . .

She looked up at the boy, her lips trembling. Inside his hood, she saw his shimmering green eyes, lined in black kohl. Then she caught a glimpse of red hair . . .

"You . . ." she said uncertainly, and slowly stood up. "How can it be?"

"Miracles happen. When you believe and desire strongly enough . . ." The young man beamed, and slowly touched the girl's lips with his own.

The girl returned an affectionate kiss. She embraced him tightly, overcome with joy.

"You still returned to me, Roziel," she whispered.

Orchidea clutched the desert rose, which hadn't faded after all these years. It hadn't faded because it was filled with her love, which never ceased.

It wasn't a dream. He had returned.

Desert Rose

About The Author

Tamuna Tsertsvadze was born in Tbilisi, Georgia. She started writing at age seven after reading Thomas Mayne Reid's *The Giraffe Hunters*. Since then, she has fallen in love with reading and writing. She wrote her first serious work when she was eleven, a 100-page story inspired by the anime Naruto, which is one of her favorite anime series. Tamuna started publishing books at the age of fourteen. Her first published work was a 179-paged work called "The Young Pirate," a story about pirates in the eighteenth century and their fight for justice.

Since then, Tamuna has been publishing her works on Amazon in English and French. In addition to English, French, and her native Georgian, Tamuna speaks Russian, Italian, German, and Spanish. She is currently learning Chinese Mandarin and Japanese. Tamuna's dream is to write books in all these languages.

At the age of seventeen, she tried her hand at screenwriting. She tried game writing as well and soon got her first job. After that, she decided to pursue game writing. She writes books and animation screenplays at the same time. Tamuna gets inspiration from everything: her dreams, daydreams, environment, nature, other authors' works, movies, and so on. For her, writing is a passion. She is happy she chose it as her path of life.

About The Publisher

Story Shares is a nonprofit focused on supporting the millions of teens and adults who struggle with reading by creating a new shelf in the library specifically for them. The ever-growing collection features content that is compelling and culturally relevant for teens and adults, yet still readable at a range of lower reading levels.

Story Shares generates content by engaging deeply with writers, bringing together a community to create this new kind of book. With more intriguing and approachable stories to choose from, the teens and adults who have fallen behind are improving their skills and beginning to discover the joy of reading. For more information, visit storyshares.org.

Easy to Read. Hard to Put Down.

www.ingramcontent.com/pod-product-compliance
Lightning Source LLC
Chambersburg PA
CBHW071225170626
46809CB00005BA/1942